Meet Me in the Middle

THIS IS A VERY SPECIAL BOOK. **IT'S A FLIP BOOK!**
THAT MEANS YOU CAN START THE STORY FROM THIS
SIDE OR FLIP IT OVER AND READ IT THE OTHER WAY. WE
HOPE YOU AGREE THAT IT'S A UNIQUE WAY OF TELLING
A STORY—AND FUN NO MATTER WHERE YOU START.

ENJOY!

GARY VAYNERCHUK

Scan to discover the world of **VeeFriends**
and all the characters featured in this book!

Meet Me in the Middle
Text copyright © 2024 by Gary Vaynerchuk
Illustrations copyright © 2024 by Vee Friends, LLC
Illustrations by Steve Lambe
All rights reserved. Manufactured in Italy.
No part of this book may be used or reproduced in any manner whatsoever without written permission
except in the case of brief quotations embodied in critical articles and reviews. For information address
HarperCollins Children's Books, a division of HarperCollins Publishers, 195 Broadway, New York, NY 10007.
www.harpercollinschildrens.com

Library of Congress Control Number: 2024931377
ISBN 978-0-06-332029-1

The artist used Adobe Photoshop 2024 and classical paint textures to create the illustrations for this book.
Design by Rick Farley
24 25 26 27 28 RTLO 10 9 8 7 6 5 4 3 2 1

First Edition

Patient Pig
Patience Pays Off

HARPER
An Imprint of HarperCollinsPublishers

Patient Pig wakes up.

"Today is the big basketball game," she says. She's ready to play her best. But first . . .

"Breakfast is the most important meal of the day," says Patient Pig.

And then: Patient Pig knows it's important to double-knot—no, triple-knot!—her shoes tight when she's going to be running around.

Oh no! Patient Pig took so long getting ready that she missed the bus. Now she's going to be late to the game.

Patient Pig has to walk to the playground, and by the time she gets to the court, the game has already started.

"Hey, look," yells Eager Eagle, "it's Patient Pig! She made it!" He waves her into the game. She might be late, but everyone can see that she's ready to play!

Headstrong Honey Badger has the ball, but Cynical Cat is guarding him.

Patient Pig makes a move to get open!

But before she can call for the ball, Eager Eagle jumps up and down and shouts, "I'm open! I'm open! Over here! Over here!"

Honey Badger passes the ball to Eager Eagle, who shoots . . . and scores!

On the next play, Patient Pig brings up the ball!

She really wants to score, but instead of shooting, she passes the ball to Thoughtful Three Horned Harpik. He scores!

Patient Pig gives him a high five. She figures she'll get another chance. But she's so patient that the game is over before she gets a chance to take a shot.

After the game, Patient Pig sees Eager Eagle heading her way.

Here he comes to tell me how many points he scored, Patient Pig thinks.

But instead, Eager Eagle gives her a fist bump. "You were *amazing*!" he says.

"No, I wasn't," Patient Pig says. "*You* were. You scored so many times!"

"You passed the ball every time someone was open. We won the game because of you! I wish I could play like you," Eager Eagle replies.

"But I wish I could play like you," Patient Pig admits.

"Maybe we can help each other," Eager Eagle says.

"I bet we can," Patient Pig agrees. "But I'm going to need your help," she tells Eagle. "Are you ready?"

"Ready?" says Eagle. "I'm not just ready—I'm *eager*!"

Eager Eagle and Patient Pig work together to build the perfect place to practice. There are cones for them to dribble around, boxes for them to jump over, baskets to shoot at, and even defenders to make it seem real.

After working hard to build it, Pig turns to her new friend and says, "It's perfect!"

"It is. It really is," Eager Eagle agrees. "Let's play!"

After hours of practicing, Patient Pig and Eager Eagle are tired and happy.

"You know," Eager Eagle tells Patient Pig, "I feel a lot better now! Your plans made this possible."

"I couldn't have done it without you," says Patient Pig. "Your excitement made me want to work harder."

"You know what—we're a great team . . ." they both agree.

"When we meet

By the time the sun is getting low in the sky, Eager Eagle and Patient Pig are worn out.

"That was so much fun," Eager Eagle says. "And all because of you."

"No," Patient Pig replies. "Because of *you*!"

"You know what—even though I'm so eager and you're so patient . . ." Eager Eagle says, and Patient Pig nods her head. He can see they're both thinking the same thing.

"We're a great team . . ." they agree.

The two friends spend the afternoon practicing their moves. Eager Eagle teaches Patient Pig to trust her instincts.

A.

0:32

B.

15

9

C.

COURSE COMPLETE!!

And Patient Pig teaches Eager Eagle not to force his shot.
"Look for the open player to try to get an easy basket."

Eager Eagle and Patient Pig work together to build the perfect place to practice. There are defenders to pass around, cones to help them find the open space, boxes for rebounding over, and even baskets to shoot at.

"This is *awesome*," Eager Eagle says.

"Let's play!" yells Patient Pig, and they're off!

"Maybe we can help each other," Eager Eagle says.

"I bet we can," Patient Pig agrees. "I've got the perfect plan in mind!"

"Let's do it!" Eager Eagle says.

"I got dizzy and tripped on my shoelace and fell and hurt my beak like a big dodo," Eager Eagle reminds Pig. "Scoring is fun, but still, sometimes I wish I could be patient and pass more."

After the game, Eager Eagle sees Patient Pig sitting on a bench.

"You were *amazing*!" he says, dapping her.

"No, I wasn't," Patient Pig says. "*You* were. You scored so many times!"

What a mess! Eager Eagle missed the steal and hurt his beak. He doesn't have the energy to even finish the game.

But in the fourth quarter,
Eager Eagle starts to slow down.
He doesn't feel so good.

Skipping breakfast was a mistake!

But Eager Eagle loves playing too
much to stop.

Adventurous Astronaut has the ball,
and Eager Eagle runs to intercept it . . .
but he drags his feet and trips over his
untied shoelace!

Eager Eagle is on fire!

Eager Eagle sprints off the bus and runs all the way to the basketball court.
Hot dog! He's the first to arrive!

Eager Eagle gets to the bus stop early and does jumping jacks until the bus arrives.

There's no time for breakfast! There isn't even time to tie his shoes! He's got a bus to catch if he's going to get to the big basketball game on time!

Eager Eagle is up and ready!

Eager Eagle

Eager to Excel!

HARPER

An Imprint of HarperCollinsPublishers